DADDY

by Jeannette Caines

Pictures by Ronald Himler

E
C
c.1

Harper & Row, Publishers
New York, Hagerstown, San Francisco, London

DADDY
Text copyright © 1977 by Jeannette Franklin Caines
Illustrations copyright © 1977 by Ronald Himler

Library of Congress Cataloging in Publication Data
Caines, Jeannette Franklin.
    Daddy.

    SUMMARY: A child of separated parents describes the special activities she shares with her father on Saturdays.
    [1. Fathers and daughters—Fiction.   2. Divorce—Fiction]   I. Himler, Ronald.
II. Title.
PZ7.C12Dad3   [E]   76-21388
ISBN 0-06-020923-2
ISBN 0-06-020924-0 lib. bdg.

My Daddy comes to get me every Saturday.
He always brings
two boxes of chocolate pudding
in a brown paper sack.

We play hide-and-seek
under the kitchen table before we leave.
Sometimes Daddy gives me money to buy new kittens—
he really means mittens.

On the way to his apartment, he always asks me,
"Windy, whose girl are you? Cindy's?"

"No, Daddy, Cindy's my dog."

"Then you must be Lamb Chops' little girl."

"Aw Daddy, you know Lamb Chops is my cat."

"Then you must be my girl, Windy."

Then he squeezes me.

When we get to his apartment,
Paula hugs me twice.
Daddy pretends he's lost his glasses—
under the couch,
behind the radiator,
in the bathroom.

But I know they're on his dresser.
When I bring them to him, he smiles at me and says,
"Paula, this Windy is the best
eyeglass finder in the world."

15

We rush to the supermarket before it closes.
Daddy and I have to read the labels to Paula—
she never wears her glasses in the street.
Sometimes we play hide-and-seek in the aisles.
Daddy buys me a coloring book with fat crayons.

When we get home,
Daddy tries to color in the lines
and breaks all the points.
But that's okay,
he promises to buy me another box next Saturday.

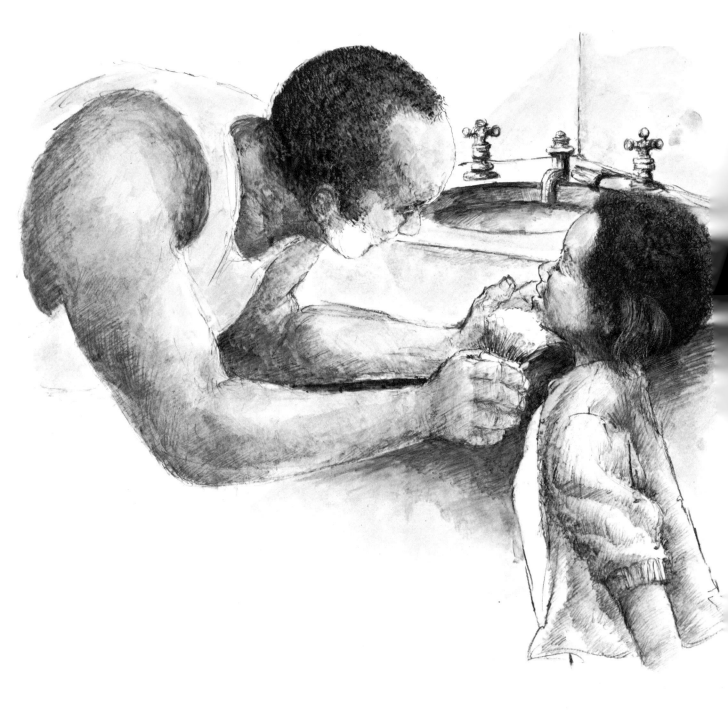

Before dinner, Daddy washes up and shaves.
He makes faces with his shaving cream
and I call him Jamie Clown.
When he makes *my* face, he calls me Sweetie Clown.

We tell Paula
we're going to cook a Saturday surprise.
She guesses three times.
Apple pie?
Sweet-potato pie?
Chocolate pudding!

Paula always has a new dress for me to try on.
"Turn around, Wind!
Stand up straight, Windy."
One Saturday she made me a wedding dress
with her old curtains,
and we put paper roses in the holes,
and then she called me Rosebud.

Today I have to stay in bed.
When Daddy came,
he took part of my medicine
so he wouldn't catch my cold.

Next Saturday when he comes
and I'm two inches taller,
we're going to fly a kite on his roof.
I know he won't forget
because he wrote our date on his calendar
and in his head.

Before Daddy comes to get me,
I get wrinkles in my stomach.
Sometimes I have wrinkles every night
and at school, worrying about him.

Then on Saturday morning
he rings one short and one long,
and my wrinkles go away.